CRAZY BIRD STORIES

Prepare yourself for Strange Birds Behaving in Strange Ways

Daryl Barnes

Illustrated by: Stephen Adams

Copyright © 2019 by Daryl Barnes

All rights reserved. This book or any portion thereof may not be reproduced or transmitted in any form or manner, electronic or mechanical, including photocopying, recording, or by any information storage or retrieval system, without the express written permission of the copyright owner except for the use of brief quotations in a book review or other noncommercial uses permitted by copyright law.

Because of the dynamic nature of the Internet, any web addresses or links contained in this book may have changed since publication and may no longer be valid. The views expressed in this work are solely those of the author and do not necessarily reflect the views of the publisher, and the publisher hereby disclaims any responsibility for them.

The Regional Arts Development Fund is a Queensland Government and Mackay Regional Council partnership to support local arts and culture.

Printed in the United States of America

Library of Congress Control Number: 2019907051
ISBN: Softcover 978-1-64376-242-5
Hardcover 978-1-64376-634-8
eBook 978-1-64376-243-2

Republished by: PageTurner, Press and Media LLC
Publication Date: 06/13/2019

To order copies of this book, contact:

PageTurner, Press and Media
Phone: 1-888-447-9651
order@pageturner.us
www.pageturner.us

Queensland
Government

DEDICATION

I dedicate this book to my mother, Melba Mona Barnes, who passed away on 10th September 2014 just short of her 95th birthday. After I was diagnosed with Parkinson's Disease in 2010, Mum encouraged me and gave me the confidence I needed to go forward and accept the challenge to beat this disease. 'I am working on it Mum'.

May she rest in peace.

STRANGE BIRDS BEHAVING IN STRANGE WAYS

It would fall over in the **street**

Then put on a squawking **show**
In a language that you wouldn't **know**

Have you **heard** of this *crazy* **bird**?
It's called the **Handsome Honeyeater**
The male spins like an **egg beater**

Performs a dance like a **world beater**
Trying to impress and to **treat her**

Have you **heard** about this **crazy** **bird**?
It's called the **Creative Crake**
It built a home out on a **lake**

Where strong winds would make it **shake**
So it set about erecting a **windbreak**

Would ride the blade of a **windmill**

Have you **heard** about this **crazy bird**?
It's called the **Navigating Nightjar**

It would follow a bright **star**
Whilst playing tunes on **guitar**

To an island with a food **bar**

Have you **heard** of this crazy **bird**?
It's called the **Sociable Silvereye**
It would search trees low and **high**

For sweet berries to make a **pie**
Then would call its friends to have a **try**

Have you **heard** about this crazy **bird**?
It's called the **Cracking Cockatoo**
It likes to have a **chew**

When it dived into swamp **muck**
And got its beak badly **stuck**

Keeping them safe in a **playpen**
And out of sight in a large **den**

Have you **heard** of this *crazy* **bird**?

It's called the **Resourceful Rail**
It built a houseboat with a **sail**

Would often crash into a street **light**

1 Lorikeet

Did you know that Rainbow Lorikeets can become disorientated and can act like they are drunk when they eat too much rich nectar? The Rainbow Lorikeet is a large brightly coloured and sometimes very noisy species. This multi coloured bird can often be seen feeding gregariously on fruit, nectar, blossoms, seeds and berries.

Rainbow Lorikeet

2 Crow

Did you know that crows and ravens can be very noisy when they get together in groups? The Torresian Crow looks very similar in appearance to all other crows and ravens in Australia. This crow has adapted well to town life and is an opportunistic scavenger of food scraps and road kills.

Torresian Crow

3 Honeyeater

Did you know that honeyeaters perform a wing flashing dance in an effort to attract a mating partner? The Eungella Honeyeater is generally found above 500 metres elevation in a 5,000 square kilometre area of the Clarke Range west of Mackay in Queensland. It constructs a nest high in the rainforest of the Eungella National Park and occupies the smallest distribution range of any bird on mainland Australia.

Eungella Honeyeater

4 Crake

Did you know that crakes construct a nest in dense reeds or grass by the shallows of a swamp or a lake? Skill, patience and some luck are required to see a crake. The White-browed Crake is typically a very secretive bird that lives along fresh water margins where there is ample cover. This small bird will venture out onto the water to feed from nearby lily pads and floating debris.

White-browed Crake

5 Spoonbill

Royal Spoonbill

Did you know that spoonbills continually move their head from side to side as they wade through the shallows of wetlands? There are two species of spoonbills in Australia. The royal, with a black bill, and the yellow-billed both search for food with their spoon shaped bills slightly open to catch crustaceans, insects and tiny fish. These birds can travel long distances soaring at a great height to find new feeding grounds.

6 Nightjar

Australian Owlet-nightjar

Did you know that the White-throated Nightjar becomes active after dark feeding on insects caught in flight? All nightjars, like owls, are night feeders and so are rarely seen during daylight hours. However, you may discover the tiny Australian Owlet-nightjar in a tree hollow with its large eyes peering out at you.

Silvereye

7 Silvereye

Did you know that Silvereyes can be found feeding in small or large groups seeking soft fruits and berries? This small bird enjoys most habitats within its range, from on or near ground level to high up in the tree-tops, where they search for food. Southern sub-species migrate north once the summer breeding is complete, to escape the cold winter weather.

Sulphur-crested Cockatoo

8 Cockatoo

Did you know that cockatoos have strong destructive curved beaks that can open nuts but can also cause damage to power poles and timber dwellings? Cockatoos are members of a very distinct and very Australian family of birds. As with most of the cockatoo species, the Sulphur-crested Cockatoo has a loud penetrating call which is often heard as they fly overhead or congregate in flocks.

Pink-eared Duck

9 Duck

Did you know that pairs of Pink-eared Ducks have been observed head to head and spinning in a circle creating a whirlpool to obtain food? Like all duck species, the Pink-eared Duck is never far from water. It is easily distinguished from other duck species by its striped flanks, a unique bill, a dark eye patch and conspicuous pink spot behind the eye.

10 Fairy-wren

Red-backed Fairy-wren

Did you know that one male fairy-wren can support a family of two or more females and several immature birds? These spectacular little birds are easily recognised by their upright tails. The male Red-backed Fairy-wren is the only species not to have any blue colouring in its plumage. The brilliant red sash on the jet black body of the male makes this bold little bird very easy to spot when he moves about the undergrowth, usually accompanied by his family that are light brown in colour.

11 Rail

Buff-banded Rail

Did you know that rails weave grasses, reeds or rushes to construct very sturdy nests? Like members of the crake family, rails rarely fly. The Buff-banded Rail has the most widespread distribution of the three rail species in Australia. It can be elusive to spot amongst dense vegetation around wetlands, lakes, rivers, coastal lagoons and sewerage farms.

12 Kite

Brahminy Kite

Did you know that all kites have excellent eye sight and can glide effortlessly for hours when searching for food? Adult Brahminy Kites are easily recognised from all other kites by their white head and chest. It generally prefers a coastal environment around the northern half of Australia where it is an opportunistic feeder, gliding along shorelines, mangroves and mudflats in search of carrion, small fish and marine creatures.

*To learn more about Australian birds, information can be obtained from any of the Field Guide publications that are readily available.

ACKNOWLEDGEMENTS

This book would not have been possible without support and encouragement from my wife, Heather and daughter, Kate.

In compiling this book I sought the help of a fellow birder and local photographer, Marlis Schoeb, who supplied me with the required bird images.

View more on her website:
www.birds-wildlife-australia.smugmug.com

Thank you to the members of Birdlife Mackay, in particular Marj Andrews and Tess Brickhill, for sharing their wealth of knowledge.

Thanks also to the Mackay Regional Council for having confidence in my project and thus providing me with a Regional Arts Development Fund grant.

Lightning Source UK Ltd.
Milton Keynes UK
UKHW050745021222
413096UK00003BA/45